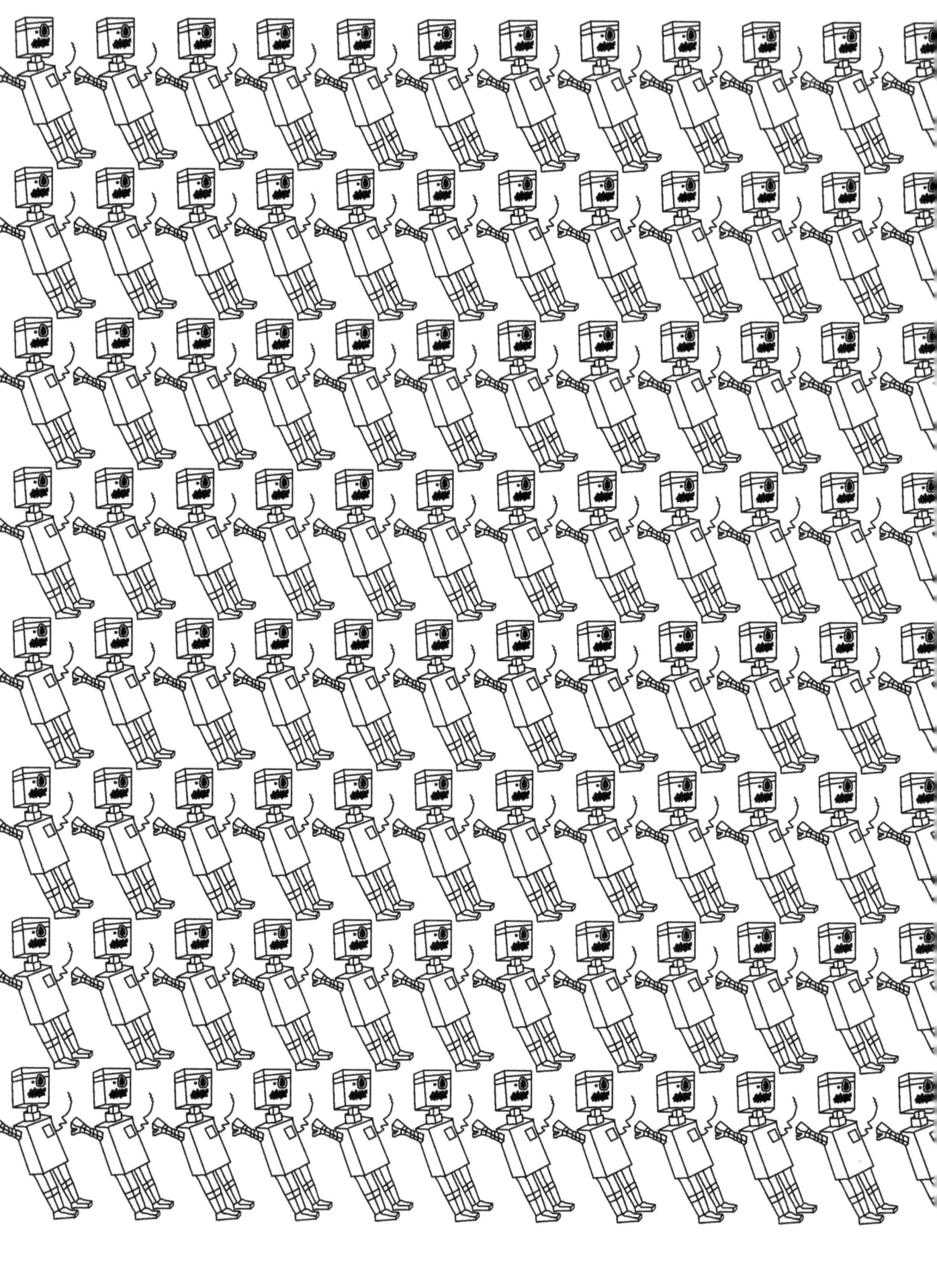

This Is Me Now

Story
&
Illustrations

By

Ms. Kimms

THIS IS ME NOW
Copyright © 2021 Erin Kimmins

All Rights reserved. No part of this book may
be used or reproduced in any manner whatsoever without written
permission. Requests to MsKimms.writes@gmail.com

For Diane.
Keep trying your best!

Diane the Robot,
Is left feeling hazy.
She was just with friends,
Playing wild and crazy.

Her feet left the sand,
As she dove for the ball.
Sadly she missed it,
And took an awkward fall.

Her arm seems strange now;
Mangled by kinks and twists.
She tries to bend it,
But it only resists.

Again and again,
She tries to change the shape.
How could this happen,
From such a small mistake?

Exasperated,
She crinkles her small brow.
The gaze in her eyes,
Questions, "This is me now?"

She stops to reflect,
About where she'll fit in.
Everything hurts her.
Her robot skin feels thin.

To make matters worse,
She hears a child whisper.
Although it's unclear,
She knows it's about her.

The mom tells her son,
"It's impolite to stare."
He answers loudly,
"But her arms aren't a pair."

Shocked by the boy's words,
She scrunches her eyebrows.
"I feel like a freak.
It's true, this is me now."

Her eyes are cast down,
As she slowly walks home.
She's empty inside,
And feeling so alone.

It's scary right now,
With an arm so mangled.
Squeaking and jerking,
It's useless and angled.

She takes a deep breath,
And then looks up ahead.
There's her friend Porkchop,
This sight lessens her dread.

He saunters over,
Sweetly crying, "Meow."
He'll help me forget,
Fearing this is me now.

Clever and funny,
He's never one to mock.
But his tail contorts,
Giving Diane a shock.

He's being so cruel,
Diane thinks to herself.
My friend is proving,
I'll be put on a shelf.

Tears begin falling,
From the sad robot's face.
Now Porkchop can see,
His friend needs an embrace.

"Did something happen?
Did someone push you down?"
Diane turns away.
Sobbing, "This is me now."

He watches his friend,
Walking sadly away.
All that Porkchop wants,
Are the right words to say.

Instead, he stands still,
Wanting to give her space.
Wishing he could help,
Sorrow clouding his face.

Diane just can't see,
That her friend is all heart.
She starts to believe,
Her life is torn apart.

No one will see me,
For the things I achieve.
They will only see,
There is something to grieve.

Diane is perplexed.
Doesn't understand how,
She'll navigate life.
"I guess, this is me now."

Later in the day,
She tries to exercise.
It might clear her head,
Of the torment inside.

Her mind is whirling.
She doesn't want to be,
Struggling with life,
Or treated differently.

Sweat is now beading,
And she starts to relax.
But only briefly,
As she's stopped in her tracks.

Alarmed by a man,
Speeding by on his bike.
"Get out of my way!"
The man growls with dislike.

Her heart is racing,
She was almost run down.
"There's no place for me.
I hate this is me now".

Tossing and turning,
Diane can't get to sleep.
Her mind's a movie—
It won't help to count sheep.

Replaying her fall,
Porkchop, biker, and kid,
The scenes from today,
Swirl behind her eyelids.

This endless cycle,
Keeps her up most the night.
She hears a bird chirp,
And sees beams of sunlight.

Yesterday was hard,
Yet she's hopeful somehow
"Things could get better.
I doubt this is me now."

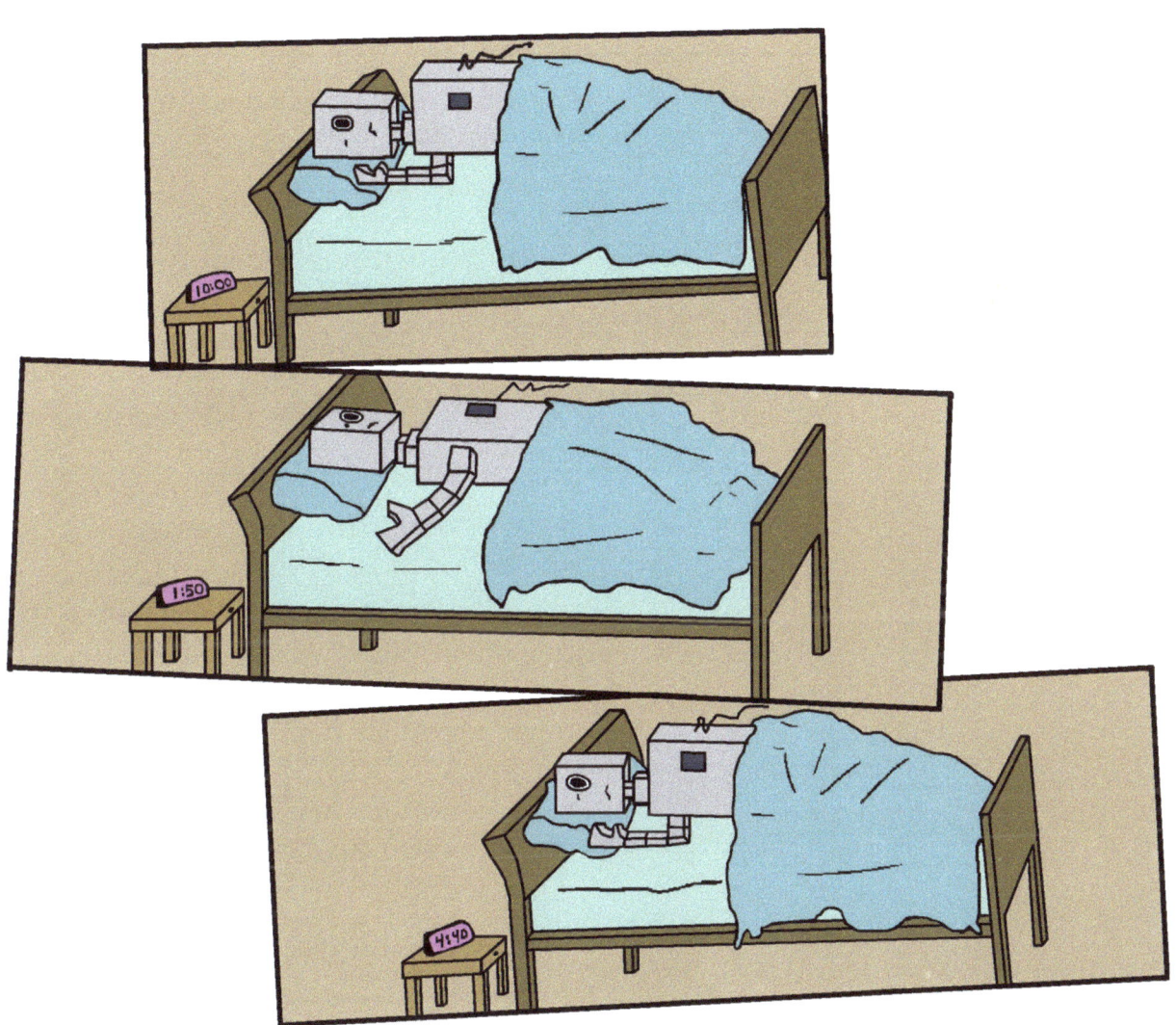

She gets up weary,
But she's willing to try.
Eggs can't be too hard.
Maybe she can get by.

A little oil spills,
A few eggshells fall in.
Not too bad a start,
She thinks with a slight grin.

Things change in a flash,
And the pan is ablaze.
She fumbles about.
Snuffs it out in a craze.

Burnt eggs in the pan,
The air heavy with smoke.
What is happening?
Is this all a bad joke?

She heads to the beach,
Not hungry, anyhow.
She slams the front door,
Screams out, "This is me now!"

Lying on the sand,
Head rests on her backpack,
She's angry and scared,
Feeling so out of whack.

Diane wants some help,
But she's unsure from who.
Does she know someone,
Who's struggled with life too?

She closes her eyes,
Listening to waves break.
She soon falls asleep,
A reprieve from heartache.

With her mind at rest,
She may figure out how,
To live her best life,
Dreaming, *This is me now.*

From far up above,
A bird watches closely.
She thinks she can help,
So she descends slowly.

Diane's eyes open.
A bird's perched on her arm.
"How rude," Diane says.
But the bird means no harm.

"I've watched you struggle,"
The bird says to Diane.
"Perhaps I might help.
I believe that I can."

"You think you can help?
How could you anyhow?"
Skeptically asking,
"You see this is me now?"

Feeling quite leery,
Of this tiny strange bird,
Diane sighs aloud,
Thinking, *This is absurd.*

The bird spreads her wings,
Giving Diane a shock.
"I know all about,
Dealing with a hard knock."

"One awkward landing,
Changed life in an instant.
Try learning to fly,
With a wing that is bent.

"I struggled alone.
It was quite hard, indeed.
You must keep trying,
And one day you'll succeed."

The bird flaps her wings,
Hovers with ease somehow.
"I once was broken.
Take a look at me now."

Diane feels lighter,
Helped by a kind stranger.
Patience and kindness,
Will guide me to answers.

Of course this is hard,
But I have to persist.
And soon I will find,
A new way to exist.

Her blue heart beats red,
Her mind filling with hope.
I will try new ways,
And not wallow or mope.

Challenges will come,
But her heart is not scarred.
I will not give up,
Even when life seems hard.

I think I can see,
Myself figuring how,
To make a great life,
Oh, yes! This is me now.

Diane wastes no time,
Trying breakfast anew.
She wants to eat scones,
With large berries so blue.

Her steps are bouncy,
And the sun makes her glow.
"I will get through this,
I don't mind if it's slow."

She pokes the large scone,
Sitting at her table.
She is determined,
Not a bit unstable.

Diane is content,
No furrow on her brow.
"My arm is a fork!"
She laughs, "This is me now."

With comfort and ease,
She fits into a crowd.
Look at her cheering —
She's very loud and proud.

As the days pass by,
Diane's confidence grows.
Sometimes she struggles —
Doesn't everyone though?

She's clearly able,
To enjoy life fully.
She no longer is,
Her own personal bully.

Kinder to herself,
She's now a deal stronger.
Finding persistence,
She fears failure no longer.

As Diane walks home,
She hears a faint meow.
I hope that's Porkchop,
He'll see this is me now.

She's happy to see,
Her little furry friend.
Porkchop says sorry,
He didn't mean to offend.

The robot accepts,
Water under the bridge.
"Please don't you worry,
Even a little smidge."

And so the Robot,
Launches into her tale.
A kind, wise stranger,
Taught Diane she's not frail.

"From that point onward,"
Diane says with a bow.
"I'm happy and free.
Grateful, this is me now!"

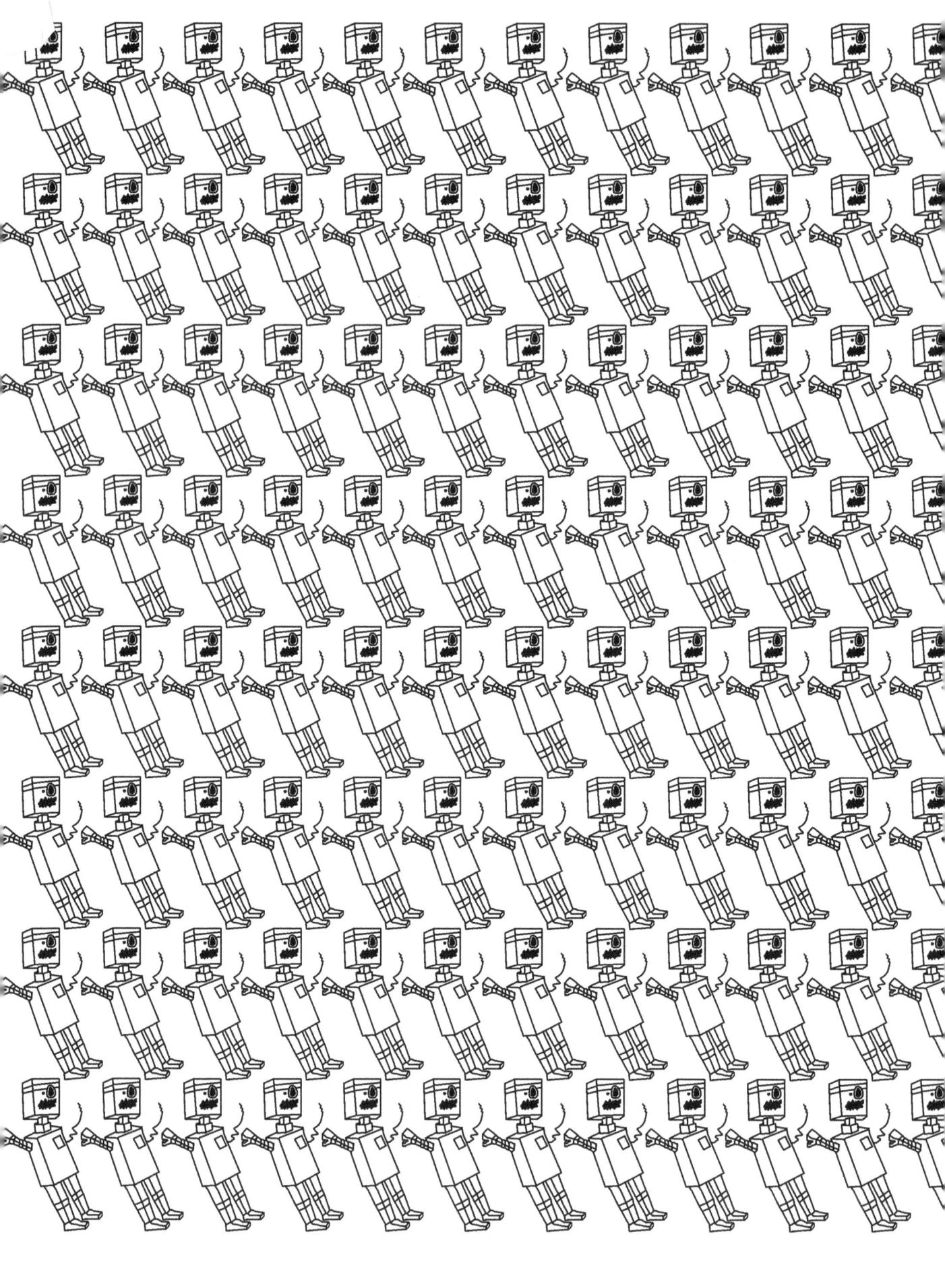

Ms. Kimms lives by the ocean. Upon her sandy perch she finds inspiration from, at times the smallest, observations of humans living life.

Ms. Kimms enjoys highlighting the, sometimes hard to find, beauty of life's great adventure.

Love being helpful? Write a review so others can find this book.

Keep your eyes peeled for upcoming stories!

What could possibly be dramatic about a birthday? Find out! It's a wild ride...

CPSIA information can be obtained
at www.ICGtesting.com
Printed in the USA
BVHW020756101121
621184BV00005B/203